Samantha Salisbury Worthington

By Denise Privette Sherman

Illustrated by Betty S. Privette

© 2002 by Denise Privette Sherman

Illustrations by Betty S. Privette

All rights reserved

Book design by: Tonya Beach

Printed in South Korea

Library of Congress Control Number: 2002108838

ISBN 0-9722221-0-3

To request additional copies write:

Wordsmith Press

3200 Milton Road

Raleigh, N.C. 27609

or call: 919-782-3665

or go to dsherman.home.mindspring.com.

Samantha

Salisbury

Worthington

For my son, John; my nieces, Anna and Kate Perko, Breece Sherman;

my nephews, Andy, Walt and Peter Hinnant, Will and Ben Caudron;

and my special friend, Ashley Malpass.

Samantha looked down at her fingers and toes.

She looked at her ears, her mouth and her nose.

"I'm tired," she said to Willow the tree,

"Of looking and talking and acting like me.

Maybe there's something else better to be.

Samantha Salisbury Worthington, Yuck!

I think I would rather quack like a duck!"

Now Willow was very big, green and wise.

Her knowledge surpassed even her size.

With a wisdom beyond her cambium rings,

She knew what such a discontent brings.

"Ahh," said Willow, all green and serene,

"Tired of yourself and such a young thing."

She then sighed a sigh that made her leaves sing.

"Samantha," she said, "Why not be you?

Be who you are — quite a big task to do."

"Oh, Willow, you are not helping at all.

I'm much too short. I want to be tall.

I think I'll become a tree just like you

If only you'll tell me what I must do.

A tree...Oh how wonderfully, marvelously grand...

A long wooden branch instead of a hand.

My head would no longer be burdened with bows,

'Cause leaves would replace them in many long rows."

Samantha did not take Willow's advice.

Being a girl just wouldn't suffice.

She dug two holes where she planted her feet.

She spread out her arms, then tucked in her seat.

Samantha Salisbury Worthington stood.

She waited for girl to turn into wood.

She waited for treetops to sprout from her head,

Where birds could make her new branches their bed.

But wooden Samantha never became...

Just real stiff from standing and from more of the same.

"I'm tired of this standing, of waiting for me

To turn myself into a big tree.

Maybe I'll change into some forest creature

If I can just find a willing, wise teacher."

Before Samantha was out of Willow's shade

A bird made a nest and sat down to rest.

This bird was the strangest Samantha had seen

In colors red, pink, yellow, purple and green.

A big gold medallion hung down on his breast.

His unruffled feathers showed part of his chest.

"I'm Sebastian Cockacanary the third,

The coolest of those that people call bird.

My grandfather of the Cockatoo brood

Read the best books and ate the best food.

The Cardinal, Canary and Toucan name

Have brought my family fortune and fame.

They fly South each winter to a place where it's hot.

In Springtime they fly to where hot it's not.

My life is one of pleasure and ease

I'm free to do whatever I please.

My latest adventure is really quite grand.

I'm the lead singer in a rock 'n roll band."

"Oh, how wonderfully, marvelously neat

To be cool as a bird, like wow, what a treat!

I'll turn my color to one rather green

Then no one will know it's me that they've seen."

"You?...Be a bird?!?!

Why, that is absurd!" said Sebastian Cockacanary the third.

"It's true that a bird is marvelously neat.

Your appraisal of us is quite on the beat.

But I, Sebastian Cockacanary,

Find your assumption extraordinary.

You?...Turn into fowl?"

Sebastian's face started to scowl.

"Stupid, preposterous, idiotic and dumb

To think you could be what I have become.

Humph, for a human to turn into bird..

Highly distasteful!!! Entirely absurd."

Sebastian the third flew away rather mad

Leaving Samantha Worthington sad.

But not for long would her quest go remiss

For she set out like a Columbus named Chris.

"Hills, mountains, valleys, across I will hike.

To find what it is that I should be like."

Samantha was tromping through the woods on her trip

When a hysterical ant hopped up on her lip.

He was jumping and shaking and screaming real shrill:

"Turn round human being, retreat if your will!"

He jumped from her lip, up to her nose

And made his pleas in eloquent prose.

"I beseech thee girl-person change your swift course

for Mound Olympus lies over yonder hill."

"Stop your prose and please speak in verse

Your prose is too hard and a turn for the worse."

"Excuse my speech (but rhyme takes time)

And I've no time to waste.

I must save my home so I work with haste!

I'm Atrium Ant, defender of mounds,

Maintainer of safety for all the ant grounds.

But if your feet keep going in this same direction

Our ant hill Olympus will have no protection.

Now don't get me wrong — there are many ant soldiers.

But small ant defenses can't fight feet like boulders.

You'd smash our nest to the ground — Flat!!!

And we have many ants who wouldn't like that."

"Oh, goodness," said Sam.

"I'll stop where I am.

Perhaps you could take me to see

If your kind is a sort that I'd like to be."

So Atrium stood on Sam Worthington's head

Both marched in time while Atrium led.

He directed Samantha to "over yonder hill"

Where below an ant colony seemed peaceful and still.

"An ant — oh how marvelously, wonderfully grand

To be an ant and play in the sand.

Atrium, could I talk to your queen

To ask if I can make the ant scene?"

Atrium Ant liked Sam a lot

"Maybe you and the queen could share the same spot.

Our queen's Cleopatra from a land far away

I hope that she'll like you and want you to stay."

But Atrium didn't understand power.

And soon his plan began to turn sour.

Four workers carried a bed up on poles.

To make Cleo happy were all of their goals.

Some other ants followed right by her side.

They fanned her and fed her — a real royal ride.

"Samantha," Cleo said. "I heard your request.

All I can say is that surely you jest.

If you think that my queendom we'll share,

You think again," she said with a stare.

"It's mine. It's all mine. It's mine through and through.

(Besides, there's no room on my throne for you.)

Two queens wouldn't work," Cleo said with a hiss.

"Cause one would say that and one would say this."

"Queen Cleopatra, I don't mean to cause trouble.

I'm not asking to become your double

If one queen more is an extra too great,

I'll become any kind of ant on this date."

"Oh, well in that case, without delay,

I'll call the professor to see what he'll say."

Professor Author O'Poda came

Up from below at the call of his name.

He was the queen's advisor-in-chief.

His knowledge provided aid and relief.

A social scientist (that's his full title)

He helped plan the mound which made their lives vital.

Ancient Greek cities and Roman ones too

Are the ones that he studied to learn what to do.

And using the best from each to date,

He created the perfect social scientist's state.

"Professor," the queen said to the brain.

"Are Samantha Worthington's wishes a pain?

She wishes to become an ant.

Is this within your power to grant?"

"To what extent can girl become ant?

Hmmm, quite a lot that you ask me to grant.

That's a big task for an academician.

Sometimes I wish I had been a beautician."

After thinking and thinking and thinking again,

The little professor started to grin.

"To what extent can girl become ant?

Very little extent, you see, she just can't.

It would mess up my balanced environmental scheme.

And what we have now is a social scientist's dream!

I'll give you an easier reason she can't

She's just too big to become an ant.

Her head is too fat to get in the mound.

She'd wreck all our pathways down in the ground."

Samantha thanked them, then bid them goodbye.

But very soon after, she started to cry.

"Will I ever find what I can be?

Will I ever be anything better than me?"

A butterfly flew down by her side.

Her eyes were young, open and wide.

"Excuse me Samantha, I don't mean to be bold.

But surely the answer you ask for's been told.

Why don't you be just who you are?

If you can do that you'll surely go far.

Let life be the teacher.

You can learn from each feature."

"It sounds real good but looks like a lie

Cause you weren't always a sweet butterfly!

A worm's life — how yucky. I see why you switched

To a butterfly. (The worm's life you ditched.)"

"I've had enough of this abuse...

If I don't speak now, I have no excuse!

You see, I thought it rather neat

To crawl around in size petite."

"Then why did you switch

If your life was so rich?"

"I was who I was and as far as I see

I really liked living my life as me.

When I was a caterpillar, I did as I should.

I lived my life the best that I could.

I made my cocoon, a house for cold seasons

And woke up a butterfly, not knowing the reasons.

So be who you are.

It's fun and it's true...

Who knows, you may be a butterfly too."

Samantha thought about her advice

More than one time she'd heard this, more than once, even twice.

She thought and she thought. She thought hard and deep.

She realized her self was someone to keep.

"I've traveled and looked about and around

I've looked in the trees, in the air, on the ground.

But I've never looked inside of me

To find who it is that I should be.

Maybe you don't need to go away very far...

To live is to learn just who you are.

I'll find who lives underneath all these bows.

Who lives 'neath this hair and all of these clothes.

I'm going to tell Willow the tree.

She'll be proud now that I see."

Willow still stood, big tall and wise.

She looked at Sam — at the gleam in her eyes.

"Samantha," she said, "I'll bet you now know

That you should be you and run your own show."

"You've known all along that I should be me

Why didn't you try harder to make me see.

I could have known and not spent this time

On searches and wishes or on words and rhyme."

"Sam, those things I said, but you couldn't be shown.

Those kind of lessons you learn own your own."

"Besides when you started, you asked how to be me...

And if I'd told you how...You'd now be a tree."